WARRIORS

SKYCLAN & THE STRANGER

THE STRANGER

#2: BEYOND THE CODE

WARRIORS
SKYCLAN & THE STRANGER
#2: BEYOND THE CODE

CREATED BY
ERIN HUNTER

WRITTEN BY
DAN JOLLEY

ART BY
JAMES L. BARRY

HARPER
An Imprint of HarperCollinsPublishers

ISBN 978-0-06-200837-4
Library of Congress Cataloging-in-Publication Data is available.

15 CG/BV 10 9 8 7 6
❖

Dear readers,

Welcome to the second part of the SkyClan manga trilogy. Leafstar has kits! I have a weakness for baby animals of any kind, but in manga they are a particular treat because I get to see my characters leaping around in the illustrations. If you've read *Bluestar's Prophecy*, you'll know that poor Bluefur felt as if she was forced to choose between her kits and her career when she was on the brink of becoming ThunderClan's deputy. But here in SkyClan, there is nothing to stop Leafstar from becoming a mother. She has a kind mate, a skilled medicine cat, and supportive senior warriors—even Sharpclaw, whose tongue can be as barbed as his talons!

Of course, raising three lively kits while leading a Clan is never going to be easy. Almost as soon as this story begins, Leafstar is torn between tending to her son's scratched nose and dealing with a problem reported by a hunting patrol. Later, her loyalties are divided even more dramatically in the thick of a battle, when she has to balance the safety of her kits with fighting alongside her Clanmates. I wanted to show that Leafstar can never stop being a mother, which means that her role as the leader of SkyClan is going to be even more difficult than before. But Leafstar has a huge heart and a great deal of courage, so I hope this is one more challenge that she relishes.

On the other hand (or paw), we have Sol. Never has a cat been more desperate to become a warrior! In this story we get to travel back to his kithood, to his unhappy mother and neglectful father, where stories of mysterious "Sky Warriors" made young Sol wish he could find his own way to escape his mother's lonely and miserable life. It's not surprising that SkyClan seems to be exactly what he has been looking for. But do all cats *deserve* to be warriors? Is it enough just to want something badly? And what about Leafstar's part in his destiny? She has the power to grant Sol's wish, and she knows how much this means to him. I wonder if you will agree with her decision. . . .

Best wishes always,
Erin Hunter

BETTER THAN BECOMING LEADER OF SKYCLAN.

SOMETIMES I EVEN WONDER IF THEY ARE MORE IMPORTANT.

I KNOW WHAT MY HEART TELLS ME. BUT MY HEART AND MY HEAD DON'T ALWAYS GET ALONG.

I WATCH THEM PLAY. THEY'RE SO TINY, SO FRAGILE.

AND PART OF ME HOPES THEY NEVER HAVE TO GO INTO BATTLE.

WHAT AM I THINKING?

THEY'RE DESTINED TO BE WARRIORS.

9

SOL'S BEEN A GOOD ADDITION TO THE CLAN.

LEARNING FAST ABOUT HUNTING AND PATROLLING THE BORDER... ESPECTFUL TO THE EXPERIENCED WARRIORS...

IF ONLY INCREASING OUR NUMBER WERE ALWAYS THAT EASY.

SPEAKING OF BEING RESPECTFUL, BIRDPAW AND HONEYPAW COULD USE A LESSON OR TWO.

WELL. LOOKS AS IF OUR YOUNG APPRENTICES DIDN'T ENJOY REMOVING TICKS FROM THE ELDERS' COATS THIS MORNING.

CAN'T IMAGINE WHY.

LICHENFUR SAID I WAS CLUMSY AS A TURTLE. SHE DIDN'T HAVE TO SAY THAT.

SOL DOESN'T HAVE TO DO APPRENTICE DUTIES. I NEVER SEE HIM PICKING TICKS.

IT'S NOT FAIR.

YEAH!

YOU BOTH KNOW SOL ISN'T EXACTLY AN APPRENTICE.

HE MAY HAVE JOINED SKYCLAN RECENTLY, BUT HE'S FULL-GROWN AND HAS LOTS OF EXPERIENCE.

EVEN IF HE HASN'T DONE WARRIOR TRAINING.

THEN HE SHOULD HAVE A WARRIOR NAME.

DON'T WORRY, HONEYPAW. HE WILL SOON.

IT'S BEEN HOT LATELY. VERY HOT. I DON'T KNOW THAT I CAN REMEMBER THE LAST TIME IT FELT LIKE THIS, FOR THIS LONG.

IT'S UNCOMFORTABLE, THAT'S CERTAIN, BUT THE EFFECTS GO BEYOND THAT.

THANKS TO THE HEAT, THE FRESH-KILL IS SCARCE...

...BECAUSE ALL THE PREY SEEMS TO BE SPENDING DAYTIME IN BURROWS OR NESTS TO AVOID THE SUN.

THIS GIVES RISE TO A PRICKLY SITUATION WITH OUR DAYLIGHT-WARRIORS...

...CATS WHO HUNT WITH US DURING THE DAY, BUT GO TO THEIR TWOLEG HOMES AT NIGHT.

THEIR SOURCES OF FOOD ARE GUARANTEED...AND IT LOOKS AS THOUGH, IN THIS HEAT...

...THEY'D RATHER BASK IN THE SUN THAN DO ANYTHING ABOUT THE DWINDLING FRESH-KILL PILE.

EVEN MY DAYLIGHT-WARRIOR MATE, BILLYSTORM, DOESN'T SEEM TOO ENTHUSIASTIC ABOUT GOING OUT ON ANOTHER PATROL.

HMMPH. "DAYLIGHT-WARRIORS."

WHAT WAS THAT, ROCKSHADE? DID YOU WANT TO SAY SOMETHING?

SURE--HOW ABOUT THIS? "WHY DON'T YOU START PULLING YOUR WEIGHT AROUND HERE FOR ONCE?"

13

JUST BECAUSE YOUR BELLIES ARE FILLED WITH KITTYPET SLOP EVERY NIGHT DOESN'T MEAN THE REST OF THE CLAN SHOULD GO HUNGRY!

ROCKSHADE... THAT'S--

HEY, YOU KNOW WHAT? THAT'S FINE. I WON'T EAT ANYTHING IF THAT'LL MAKE YOU HAPPY.

YEAH, IT WOULD, ACTUALLY.

I BET TWO OF US COULD LIVE ON THE FOOD YOU GOBBLE DOWN EVERY DAY.

I DIDN'T REALIZE MY EATING HABITS UPSET YOU SO MUCH.

MAYBE I JUST WON'T EVEN BOTHER TURNING UP AT ALL?

THAT'D SUIT ME JUST FINE.

CLAN CATS SNAPPING AT EACH OTHER LIKE THIS MAKES MY HEAD POUND...

...AND IT'S HAPPENING MORE AND MORE AS THE HEAT WEARS ON.

14

THEY'RE JUST FRAZZLED AND FRUSTRATED. I KNOW THEY DON'T MEAN THE THINGS THEY SAY.

BUT STILL, I'D BETTER GO AND PUT A STOP TO IT BEFORE ANYTHING BAD HAP--

I'LL GET YOU!

OH! UH...UH...

MEEEEEP!

HARRYKIT! WHAT HAPPENED?

MY NOSE! MEEEEEEP! MEEEEEEP!

MEEEEEEEP!

A QUESTION RISES UP IN MY MIND, NOT FOR THE FIRST TIME.

SHOULD CLAN LEADERS EVER HAVE KITS?

LEAFSTAR?

SOL--WHAT IS IT?

NOTHING, I... HERE. I THOUGHT THIS MIGHT HELP.

FOR THE LITTLE ONE, I MEAN.

THERE.

SOON YOU'LL BE GOOD AS NEW.

WOW...

YOU'VE GOT A TOUGH JOB. MANAGING THESE THREE AND ALL OF US. HOW DO YOU DO IT?

OH...IT JUST TAKES PATIENCE, IS ALL. PATIENCE, AND MUCH-APPRECIATED HELP FROM MY CLANMATES.

I BET IT'S HARD TO TELL US APART FROM THE KITS SOMETIMES, ISN'T IT?

HA-HA-HA... NOT USUALLY.

LEAFSTAR...I'M SORRY I COULDN'T SETTLE THE KITS DOWN ON MY OWN.

IT'S OKAY. THEY DON'T SEEM TO BE ABLE TO TAKE TWO BREATHS WITHOUT ME AT THE MOMENT, DO THEY?

WELL, YOU'RE A BRILLIANT MOTHER. AND THEY'RE STILL YOUNG KITS. THEY'LL GET MORE INDEPENDENT WITH TIME.

AHEM...

SOL, DON'T YOU HAVE A PATROL TO GO ON?

NOT THAT I KNOW OF! WHY? DO YOU WANT TO LEAD ONE?

20

MAMA! MAMA! HARRYKIT'S NOSE IS GOING TO BE OKAY!

OH? YOU'VE DECIDED THAT, HAVE YOU?

YEAH! PLUS, WE'RE HUNGRY!

LET'S DISCUSS PATROLS AND SUCH LATER, SHALL WE?

GOOD IDEA.

OKAY.

LEAFSTAR?

HARPCLAW-- YES?

OH--UH... RIGHT.

I'M GOING TO LET THE CATS TAKE SOME TIME OUT UNTIL THE SUN IS BELOW THE TREETOPS.

THAT'S A GOOD THOUGHT. GO AHEAD.

THANKS.

THEY HAVE ENOUGH FRESH-KILL TO LAST THE DAY--NO USE STORING IT ANYWAY SINCE IT SPOILS SO FAST IN THIS HEAT.

SHARPCLAW IS A FANTASTIC DEPUTY. I'M NOT SURE HOW I WOULD HAVE MANAGED WITHOUT HIM.

BUT THEN, I GUESS THAT'S WHAT THE CLAN IS ALL ABOUT. HELPING EACH OTHE

THE DAYLIGHT-WARRIORS HEAD BACK TO THEIR TWOLEG NESTS AS THE DAY COMES TO AN END...

...EXCEPT, TODAY, FOR BILLYSTORM AND EBONYCLAW. GIVING ME ONE MORE REASON TO BE PROUD OF MY MATE.

YOU'RE DOING WHAT, NOW?

WE'LL HUNT FOR THE CLAN WITHOUT EATING FROM THE FRESH-KILL PILE.

RIGHT. WE KNOW WE'LL BE FED WHEN WE GET BACK TO OUR HOUSEFOLK. IT ONLY SEEMS FAIR.

THANK YOU. BOTH OF YOU.

IT'S THE LEAST WE CAN DO.

ALL RIGHT, I WANT THREE PATROLS, FRONT AND CENTER! WARRIORS AND APPRENTICES BOTH! MOVE!

SHARPCLAW DROPS EASILY INTO HIS ROLE OF SHOUTING ORDERS, BUT I CAN TELL... TODAY, IT HIDES HIS RELIEF.

AS LONG AS THE HEAT KEEPS UP, WE NEED ALL THE HELP WE CAN GET.

WE WANNA GO ON PATROL TOO, MAMA!

YEAH! I WANNA BRING BACK A SKIRREL!

STARCLAN HELP ME...THE KITS'VE BEEN NAPPING ALL AFTERNOON.

IT'LL BE A MIRACLE IF I GET ANY SLEEP AT ALL TONIGHT.

LOOK HOW EASILY SOL FITS IN WITH US, ECHOSONG.

I'M REALLY GLAD HE JOINED SKYCLAN.

HE SEEMS BOUND AND DETERMINED TO BE THE BEST WARRIOR EVER!

YES...BUT... WELL, WE KNOW SO LITTLE ABOUT HIM, OR WHERE HE COMES FROM.

THAT MAY BE TRUE...BUT, TO BE FAIR, I DON'T REALLY KNOW MUCH ABOUT YOUR LIFE BEFORE YOU CAME TO THE GORGE, EITHER.

THERE'S NOT MUCH TO TELL.

SO...MAYBE THE SAME GOES FOR SOL? WE HAVE TO TRUST HIM.

"THAT'S WHAT BEING A CLANMATE IS ALL ABOUT."

KEEP IT QUIET, WARRIORS.

LET'S MOVE OUT.

WE COULD TOTALLY GO ON A PATROL, MAMA!

I BET I COULD BRING BACK TWO SKIRRELS!

WELL, IF YOU'RE GOING TO GO ON PATROL, I NEED TO TEACH YOU A FEW BASICS FIRST. WHO WANTS TO LEARN TO HUNT?

MEEE! MEEE! MEEE!

OKAY. THE FIRST THING WE'LL LEARN IS HOW TO SNEAK UP ON SOMETHING. LET'S PRETEND MY TAIL IS A FOX...

QUIET! DON'T MAKE A SOUND!

I'M NOT! I'M NOT!

ROARRR!

EEEEEEEEE!

IT'S THE FOX! DON'T LET THE FOX GET ME!

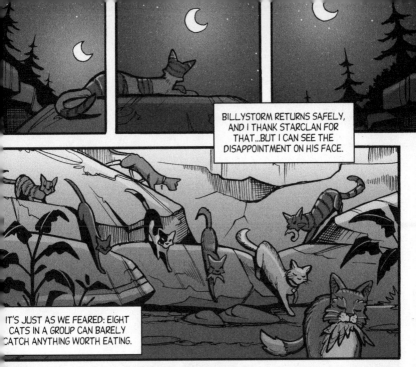

BILLYSTORM RETURNS SAFELY, AND I THANK STARCLAN FOR THAT...BUT I CAN SEE THE DISAPPOINTMENT ON HIS FACE.

IT'S JUST AS WE FEARED: EIGHT CATS IN A GROUP CAN BARELY CATCH ANYTHING WORTH EATING.

UM... WE'RE BACK, TOO.

PATCHFOOT, WHAT HAPPENED? WHERE IS EVERYONE ELSE?

WELL, SEE, SOL HAD AN IDEA...

WHAT? WHAT IDEA?

HE, UM...WELL, HE DIDN'T EXACTLY SAY. BUT HE TALKED US INTO LETTING HIM SPLIT THE PATROL IN TWO.

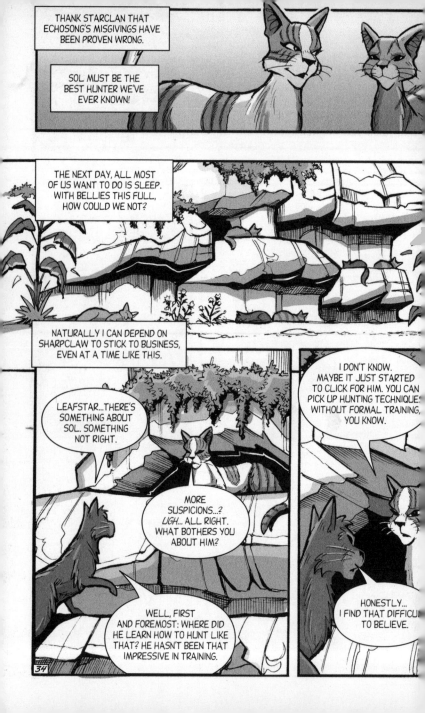

THANK STARCLAN THAT ECHOSONG'S MISGIVINGS HAVE BEEN PROVEN WRONG.

SOL MUST BE THE BEST HUNTER WE'VE EVER KNOWN!

THE NEXT DAY, ALL MOST OF US WANT TO DO IS SLEEP. WITH BELLIES THIS FULL, HOW COULD WE NOT?

NATURALLY I CAN DEPEND ON SHARPCLAW TO STICK TO BUSINESS, EVEN AT A TIME LIKE THIS.

LEAFSTAR...THERE'S SOMETHING ABOUT SOL. SOMETHING NOT RIGHT.

I DON'T KNOW. MAYBE IT JUST STARTED TO CLICK FOR HIM. YOU CAN PICK UP HUNTING TECHNIQUES WITHOUT FORMAL TRAINING, YOU KNOW.

MORE SUSPICIONS...? UGH... ALL RIGHT. WHAT BOTHERS YOU ABOUT HIM?

WELL, FIRST AND FOREMOST: WHERE DID HE LEARN HOW TO HUNT LIKE THAT? HE HASN'T BEEN THAT IMPRESSIVE IN TRAINING.

HONESTLY... I FIND THAT DIFFICULT TO BELIEVE.

WELL, NO NEED FOR IT TO BE A MYSTERY.

IT ONLY TAKES A SIMPLE REQUEST TO GET CLOVERTAIL AND HONEYPAW TO LOOK AFTER MY KITS FOR AN EVENING.

I'LL ASK SOL IF I CAN GO WITH HIM TONIGHT. I COULD DO WITH A NIGHT OUT, ANYWAY.

MAYBE I'LL LEARN SOMETHING.

HONEYPAW LOVES PLAYING GAMES WITH THEM SO MUCH, THEY PROBABLY THINK SHE'S MORE FUN THAN I AM.

SOL. I HAVE A REQUEST FOR YOU.

SURE THING, LEAFSTAR. ANYTHING YOU WANT!

I KNOW WE'RE ALL STILL FULL FROM LAST NIGHT, BUT TONIGHT I'D LIKE YOU TO LEAD ANOTHER HUNTING PATROL.

AND I'LL TAG ALONG, IF YOU DON'T MIND.

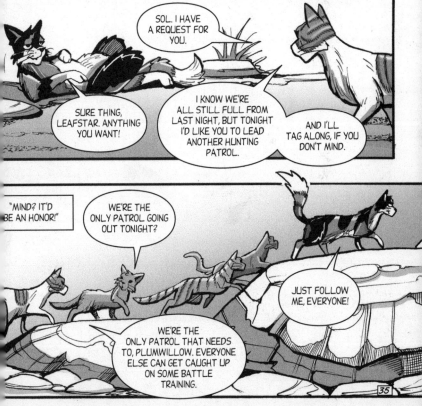

"MIND? IT'D BE AN HONOR!"

WE'RE THE ONLY PATROL GOING OUT TONIGHT?

JUST FOLLOW ME, EVERYONE!

WE'RE THE ONLY PATROL THAT NEEDS TO, PLUMWILLOW. EVERYONE ELSE CAN GET CAUGHT UP ON SOME BATTLE TRAINING.

35

THE SMELL OF THE FOXES HITS ME JUST BEFORE I HEAR THEIR PADDING FEET.

THANK STARCLAN WE'RE DOWNWIND, OR THEY'D BE ALL OVER US!

WHY AREN'T WE RUNNING AWAY?

NOW!

38

COME ON!

HE FOXES ARE BRINGING THEIR CUBS OUT OF THE DEN NOW... BRINGING THEM OUT TO FEED!

39

I CAN'T EVEN COMPREHEND WHAT JUST HAPPENED.

SEE, LEAFSTAR? IF THE FOXES WANT TO HUNT AT DUSK, WE'LL LET THEM DO OUR HUNTING FOR US AS WELL!

SOL, THIS IS--I CAN'T EVEN BEGIN TO--

THIS IS THE ABSOLUTE WORST THING YOU COULD HAVE DONE!

YOU'VE JUST LEFT A TRAIL FOR THOSE FOXES ALL THE WAY TO OUR CAMP! WHAT IF THEY COME HERE AND ATTACK US?

WHAT? ...BUT I FIGURED--

THIS IS NOT HOW CLAN CATS HUNT! THEY USE SKILLS!

BUT THIS IS A SKILL...

NO, IT'S NOT. IT'S STEALING. STEALING FROM FOXES, NO LESS! YOU MUST STOP IT AT ONCE.

THAT'S AN ORDE

ADE IT BACK, HAVE YOU? I WAS--

--WOW! WHAT A HAUL! HOW DID YOU CATCH ALL THAT?

WE DIDN'T CATCH IT. A FOX DID.

...TELL ME YOU'RE JOKING!

LOOK, IT'S FOOD, FOXES DIDN'T FOLLOW AND WE'VE GOT ENOUGH O FEED THE WHOLE CLAN USING ONLY FOUR CATS.

I DON'T SEE WHAT THE PROBLEM IS!

YOU KNOW NOTHING ABOUT THE WARRIOR CODE.

YOU'VE PUT THE WHOLE CLAN IN DANGER!

ALL RIGHT, ALL RIGHT, LET'S JUST CALM DOWN, ALL OF US.

MAYBE IT'S OKAY IF THIS IS THE LAST TIME. SOL WAS ONLY TRYING TO HELP.

NONE OF US WILL SAY ANYTHING ABOUT THIS TO THE REST OF THE CLAN.

NO USE IN UPSETTING EVERYONE IF THERE'S NO CAUSE FOR IT.

41

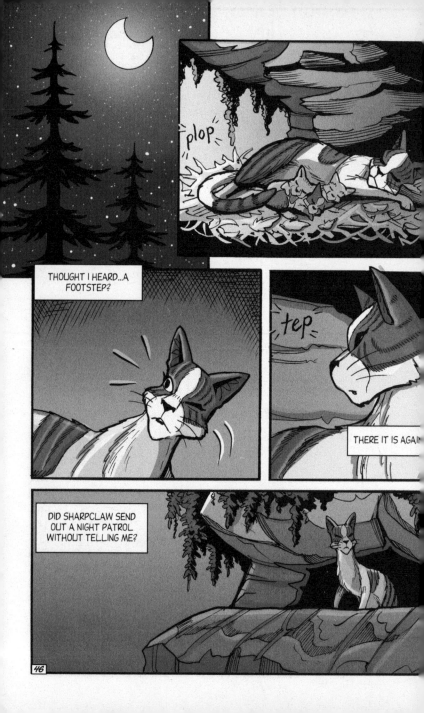

OH, NO.
OH, NO!

BUT WE COULD HAVE HELPED, MAMA!

NO, YOU COULD NOT HAVE HELPED. YOU'RE ALL STILL TOO SMALL.

BUT--

NO, NO "BUTS." IF YOU PULL A STUNT LIKE THAT AGAIN, YOU'LL GET NOTHING BUT MOUSE TAILS FOR TWO DAYS.

EAFSTAR... I...

I'M SO, SO SORRY. I JUST...

I JUST GOT SO SCARED.

AND I DIDN'T KNOW. I DIDN'T KNOW WHAT TO DO. HOW TO HELP.

WILL OU...

ARE YOU GOING TO TELL THE REST OF THE CLAN THAT IT WAS MY FAULT THE FOXES CAME?

...NO. NO, THERE'D BE NO POINT. SOL....

LISTEN, MAYBE CLAN LIFE JUST ISN'T RIGHT FOR YOU. HUNTING AND FIGHTING ARE AT THE CENTER OF BEING A CLAN WARRIOR.

IT'S NOT YOUR FAULT IF YOU'RE JUST NOT BORN WITH THE RIGHT INSTINCTS.

53

WELL, IT'S JUST NEVER GOING TO QUIT RAINING, IS IT? WE'LL ALL CATCH OUR DEATH BEFORE IT'S OVER.

NOT AS IF ANYBODY WOULD KNOW WE WERE GONE ANYWAY.

YOU CAN FORGET ABOUT THE SKY WARRIORS. THEY'RE NOT HERE NOW, ARE THEY? NO ONE IS.

OOH--MAMA? I KNOW WHAT WOULD CHEER US UP!

TELL US A STORY ABOUT THE SKY WARRIORS!

NO ONE CAN HELP US.

"FINALLY WE FOUND SOME SHELTER IN A LOG PILE. IT WAS PRETTY DRAFTY, BUT IT LET US STOP AND REST."

"AND WE ALL GOT EXCITED WHEN OUR FATHER SHOWED UP."

"THOUGH I GUESS WE SHOULD'VE KNOWN BETTER."

CINDERS.

WELL. LOOK WHO FINALLY SHOWS HIS FACE. AND FOODLESS AGAIN, NOT THAT I'M SURPRISED.

61

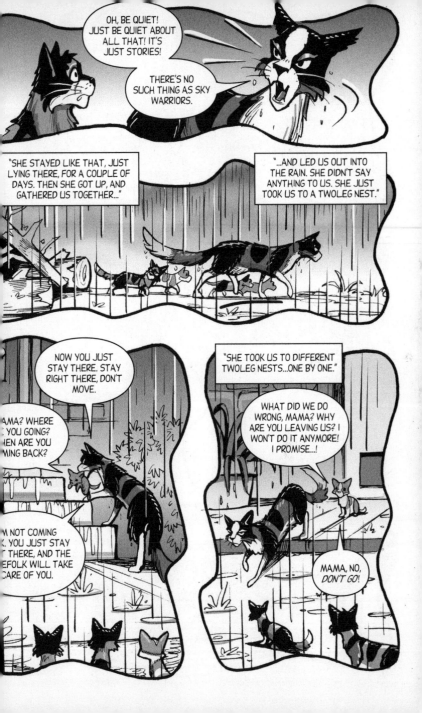

"WISHING OVER AND OVER THAT I COULD'VE BEEN A SKY WARRIOR...BECAUSE THEN SHE..."

THE OLD ONE WHO TOOK ME IN WAS KIND, AND KEPT ME WELL-FED.

"...MIGHT'VE STAYED..."

BUT WHEN YOU SHOWED UP, AND I FOUND OUT THE CLAN HAD RETURNED... I JUST...COULDN'T BELIEVE IT.

SKYCLAN WAS REAL. I'D FINALLY GET TO BE A PART OF IT!

OKAY, SO MAYBE THE CATS HERE DON'T ACTUALLY FLY OR TURN INTO LIONS...

...BUT THEY ARE BRAVE, AND HONORABLE, AND ALWAYS LOOK OUT FOR EACH OTHER. YOU SEE? MY WISH HAS COME TRUE!

WHEREVER CINDERS IS...

SHE MUST BE SO PROUD AND HAPPY TO KNOW THAT I'VE BECOME A SKYCLAN WARRIOR!

OH, SOL...

I'M SO SORRY THAT YOU LOST YOUR MOTHER AND YOUR BROTHERS AND SISTERS LIKE THAT.

BUT... BUT YOU UNDERSTAND NOW?

YOU KNOW WHY BEING A WARRIOR IS SO IMPORTANT TO ME?

SOL GAVE ME A LOT OF INFORMATION TO TAKE IN.

I'VE BEEN THINKING ABOUT IT A GREAT DEAL.

AND I NEED ME PERSPECTIVE.

SO...WHAT ARE YOUR THOUGHTS ON SOL THESE DAYS?

WELL...I WAS PRETTY HORRIFIED UT WHAT HAPPENED DURING THE FOX ATTACK.

SOL DOESN'T SEEM TO HAVE MUCH IN THE WAY OF COURAGE. OR FIGHTING TACTICS.

PLUS, JUST BEING HONEST, HE'S LAZY. AND A BIT TOO CLEVER. HE ALWAYS THINKS OF REASONS NOT TO DO SOMETHING.

I GO INTO THIS WITH GREAT HOPES...

...THAT SOL WILL CATCH ON TO WHAT I'M SHOWING HIM, AND REALLY START TO SHINE.

REALLY LOW...FLATTEN YOURSELF OUT...

BUT HE JUST...DOESN'T.

LIKE THIS?

HMMM.

AYBE IT'S BECAUSE OF HIS ONS SPENT AS A KITTYPET.

JUST STRAIGHT UP--AS HIGH AS YOU CAN.

MAYBE SHARPCLAW IS RIGHT, AND HE JUST DOESN'T HAVE IT.

LIKE THIS?

HMMM.

I'M ALMOST READY TO AGREE WITH SOL, THAT HE IS TERRIBLE AT THIS...

...WHEN HE SURPRISES ME. SURPRISES HIMSELF, TOO.

I DID IT!

HA! I DID IT! I DID IT!

A LITTLE BIT OF SUCCESS PROVES TO BE A TURNING POINT OF SORTS FOR SOL. WE START IN ON EVASION TECHNIQUES...

...AND HE DOESN'T DO HALF BAD.

THEN WE TRY THE SAME THING I TAUGHT MY KITS... SNEAKING UP ON SOMETHING SOUNDLESSLY...

...AND AGAIN, HE'S SURPRISINGLY DECENT AT IT.

SO--HOW'S MY WARRIOR TRAINING NOW, LEAFSTAR?

I CAN SAFELY SAY THAT YOU ARE LEARNING, SOL.

YOU'RE ON YOUR WAY.

EXHAUSTED BY THAT NIGHT, BUT I CAN'T SLEEP YET.

IT'S TIME FOR OUR GATHERING.

A LOT HAS HAPPENED SINCE OUR LAST ONE.

BUT I'M HOPING TO KEEP THINGS FOCUSED ON MOVING FORWARD TONIGHT...

...RATHER THAN LOOKING BACK.

THAT SHOULDN'T BE TOO HARD.

THE WIND IS SUDDENLY MUCH COLDER, AND WE ALL KNOW WHAT THAT MEANS.

SNFF SNFF RAIN'S ON THE WAY.

GOOD.

WE COULD SURE USE SOME!

HUSH, LITTLE ONES, HUSH...IT'S ALL RIGHT. IT'S JUST A STORM.

IT'S ALL RIGHT.

BUT I'M SCARED THAT IT MIGHT NOT BE "JUST A STORM."

I DON'T THINK I'VE EVER SE RAIN THIS HARD BEFORE

YOU'RE HERE! THANK STARCLAN YOU'RE ALL OKAY!

BILLYSTORM! WHAT ARE YOU DOING HERE?

WON'T YOUR HOUSEFOLK BE SCARED?

I COULDN'T LEAVE YOU ON YOUR OWN. NOT IN SUCH A BAD STORM.

EASIER TO KEEP THE KITS SAFE WITH BOTH OF US HERE.

I...

THANK YOU.

LEAFSTAR? CAN I COME IN?

WE MIGHT HAVE TO CONSIDER EVACUATING THE LOWER DENS.

YOU THINK IT'S THAT SERIOUS?

THERE ARE ALREADY SOME REALLY BIG PUDDLES FORMING AT THE BOTTOM OF THE GORGE.

WE SHOULD BE ABLE TO FIT INTO THE WARRIORS' DENS FOR THE NIGHT, THOUGH.

WE ALL FEEL IT BEFORE WE HEAR IT. A RUMBLING SOUND, DEEPER AND MORE AWFUL THAN ANY THUNDER.

RRUUMMBLE

MAMA, MAMA, WHAT'S THAT NOISE?

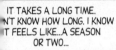

83

CATS, DAZED AND BEDRAGGLE! MAKE THEIR WAY BACK INTO WHAT'S LEFT OF OUR CAMP.

I DON'T EVEN RECOGNIZE THE FOREST BELOW THE GORGE NOW.

SO MANY TREES ARE JUST...GONE.

CAN YOU--WOULD YOU MIND LOOKING AFTER THE KITS FOR A BIT?

I NEED TO FIND OUT HOW BAD THINGS ARE.

OF COURSE.

WE'LL BE RIGHT HERE.

SKYCLAN!

I NEED ALL CATS ACCOUNTED FOR! IS ANYONE HURT?

NOTHING SERIOUS SO FAR, LEAFSTAR!

I'M BEGINNING TO THINK WE'VE GOTTEN OFF EASY, AS FAR AS PERSONAL DAMAGE GOES.

THOUGH I REALLY WISH ALL MY HERBS AND SUPPLIES HADN'T JUST BEEN WASHED AWAY!

I GUESS I SHOULD KNOW BETTER THAN TO GET TOO OPTIMISTIC.

OH, NO... NO...*NOOO*...

IT'S LICHENFUR!

SHE'S DEAD!

LICHENFUR...

NO...

KNOWN HER MY WHOLE LIFE...

...REMEMBER HOW SHE SAVED LEAFSTAR'S KITS?

LOST A HERO TODAY...

LEAFSTAR...?

COULD WE... WOULD IT BE ALL RIGHT IF WE SIT WITH HER?

FOR THE REST OF THE NIGHT, I MEAN...LIKE WE DID WITH RAINFUR?

OR...OR, I MEAN, I KNOW THE DENS ARE WRECKED...

DO YOU WANT US TO GET STARTED PUTTING THEM BACK TOGETHER INSTEAD?

FOR A HEARTBEAT MY BRAIN JUST WON'T WORK.

THERE'S SO MUCH TO DO... SO MUCH DESTROYED.

NO...NO.

THE CAMP CAN WAIT FOR A WHILE.

TONIGHT WE'LL SIT VIGIL FOR OUR LOST CLANMATE.

STARCLAN, WHY DID YOU LET THIS STORM HAPPEN?

WHY CAN'T YOU LET SKYCLAN LIVE HERE IN PEACE?

DON'T WORRY. WE'LL REBUILD THE DENS.

SKYCLAN WILL SURVIVE.

TO BE CONCLUDED

ERIN HUNTER

is inspired by a love of cats and a fascination with the ferocity of the natural world. As well as having great respect for nature in all its forms, Erin enjoys creating rich, mythical explanations for animal behavior. She is also the author of the Seekers series.

Download the free Warriors app and chat on Warriors message boards at www.warriorcats.com.

For exclusive information on your favorite authors and artists, visit www.authortracker.com.

WARRIORS

SKYCLAN & THE STRANGER

AFTER THE FLOOD

ERIN HUNTER

3

SKYCLAN'S ADVENTURES
CONTINUE IN

WARRIORS

SKYCLAN &
THE STRANGER

#3 AFTER THE FLOOD

Leafstar is struggling to keep SkyClan united in the
wake of the flood that destroyed their camp, but her
Clanmates are scared of what might happen next.
Meanwhile, Sol continues to demand that Leafstar make
him a warrior, but Leafstar isn't sure that Sol will ever
be ready to embrace the warrior code. As SkyClan faces
another devastating challenge, Leafstar must figure out
what is best for her Clan—once and for all.

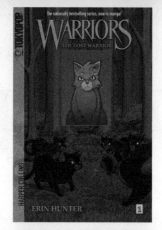

WARRIORS

THE LOST WARRIOR

WARRIOR'S REFUGE

WARRIOR'S RETURN

Find out what really happened to Graystripe when he was captured by Twolegs, and follow him and Millie on their torturous journey through the old forest territory and Twolegplace to find ThunderClan.

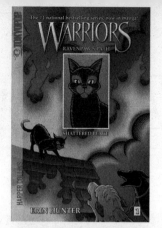

RAVENPAW FIGHTS
TO DEFEND HIS HOME IN

WARRIORS

RAVENPAW'S PATH

#1: SHATTERED PEACE

#2: A CLAN IN NEED

#3: THE HEART OF A WARRIOR

Ravenpaw has settled into life on the farm, away from the forest and Tigerstar's evil eye. He knows that leaving the warrior Clans was the right choice, and he appreciates his quiet days and peaceful nights with his best friend, Barley. But when five rogue cats from Twolegplace come to the barn seeking shelter, Ravenpaw and Barley are forced to flee their new home. With the help of ThunderClan, Ravenpaw and Barley must try to find a way to overpower the rogues—before they lose their home for good.

WARRIORS

THE RISE OF SCOURGE

TOKYOPOP®

HARPER COLLINS

ERIN HUNTER

WARRIORS

THE RISE OF SCOURGE

Black-and-white Tiny may be the runt of the litter, but he's also the most curious about what lies beyond the backyard fence. When he crosses paths with some wild cats defending their territory, Tiny is left with scars—and a bitter, deep-seated grudge—that he carries with him back to Twolegplace. As his reputation grows among the strays and loners that live in the dirty brick alleyways, Tiny leaves behind his name, his kittypet past, and everything that was once important to him—except his deadly desire for revenge.

THE #1 NATIONAL BESTSELLING SERIES

OMEN OF THE STARS

WARRIORS

THE FORGOTTEN WARRIOR

ADVENTURE GAME INSIDE!

ERIN HUNTER

TURN THE PAGE FOR A PEEK
AT THE NEXT WARRIORS NOVEL,

WARRIORS

OMEN OF
THE STARS #5

THE FORGOTTEN WARRIOR

As a full-scale battle against the Dark Forest moves closer, Jayfeather, Lionblaze, and Dovewing are desperate to prepare the four Clans to fight. But while tensions reach a breaking point, a stranger appears in ThunderClan's midst, spinning a web of deceit, and pitting the warriors against each other so that no cat can tell who to trust.

CHAPTER 1

Jayfeather's dream dissolved into darkness as he woke and stretched his jaws in a massive yawn. His whole body seemed heavy, and when he sat up in his nest he felt as though ivy tendrils were wrapped around him, dragging him back to the ground. The air was hotter than usual for late newleaf, filled with the scents of prey and lush green growth. Noise filtered through the brambles that screened the medicine cat's den from the rest of the stone hollow: pawsteps and the excited murmuring of many cats as they gathered for the first patrols of the day.

But Jayfeather couldn't share his Clanmates' excitement. Although a moon had passed since he and his companions had returned from their visit to the Tribe, he felt cold and bleak inside. His head was full of images of mountains, endless snow-covered peaks stretching into the distance, outlined crisply against an ice-blue sky. His belly cramped with pain as he recalled one particular image: a white cat with green eyes who gave him a long, sorrowful look before she turned away and padded along a cliff top above a thundering waterfall.

Jayfeather shook his head. *What's the matter with me? That was all a long, long time ago. My life has always been here with the Clans. So why do I feel as if something has been lost?*

"Hi, Jayfeather." Briarlight's voice had a muffled, echoing sound, and Jayfeather realized she must have her head inside the cleft where he stored his herbs. "You're awake at last."

Jayfeather replied with a grunt. Briarlight was another of his problems. He couldn't forget what Lionblaze had told him when he returned to the mountains: how Briarlight was so frustrated by being confined to the hollow, trapped by her damaged hindlegs, that she'd persuaded her brother Bumblestripe to carry her into the forest to look for herbs.

"There was a dog running loose," Lionblaze had told him. "A cat with four functioning legs would have been hard-pressed to outrun it. If it hadn't been for me and Toadstep luring it away, Briarlight would have been torn to pieces."

"Mouse-brain!" Jayfeather snapped. "Why would she put herself in danger like that?"

"Because she's convinced that she's useless," Lionblaze explained. "Can't you give her more to do? Cinderheart and I promised her we'd help her find a proper part to play in the life of the Clan."

"You had no right to promise her anything without speaking to me first," Jayfeather retorted. "Are you suggesting I take her as my apprentice? Because I don't want an apprentice!"

"That's not what I meant," Lionblaze meowed, his tail-tip twitching in annoyance. "But you could find more interesting duties for her, couldn't you?"

Still reluctant, Jayfeather had done as his brother asked. He had to admit that Briarlight was easy to teach. She had been stuck in the medicine cat's den for so long that she had already picked up a lot.

She's actually useful, he mused. *Her paws are neat and quick when she sorts the herbs, and she's good at soaking wilted leaves in the pool without letting them fall to pieces.*

"Jayfeather?" Briarlight's voice roused Jayfeather from his thoughts. He heard her wriggling around, and then her voice came more clearly as if she was poking her head out of the cleft. "Are you okay? You were tossing and turning all night."

"I'm fine," Jayfeather muttered, unwilling to dwell any longer on the dreams that had plagued him.

"We're running low on marigold," Briarlight went on. "We used up a lot on Dovewing's scratches when you got back from the mountains. Should I ask Brightheart to collect some more?"

"No, I'll go," Jayfeather muttered.

"Fine." Briarlight's voice was determinedly cheerful. "I'll get on with sorting the herbs. Oh, one more thing . . ."

Jayfeather heard the young she-cat dragging herself across the floor of the den until she reached his nest and pushed something toward him. "Could you throw this out on your way past the dirtplace?" she asked. "It was stuck at the back of the herb store."

Jayfeather stretched out his neck until his nose touched a tuft of fur with a few dried scraps of leaf dusted on it. He stiffened as he recognized the faint scent that clung to it.

"Who would have put an old bit of fur among the herbs?" Briarlight continued. "It must have been in there for ages. I don't recognize the scent or color."

For a moment Jayfeather didn't reply. He breathed in his lost sister's scent, overwhelmed by longing for the time when he and Hollyleaf and Lionblaze had played and trained together, before they knew anything about the prophecy, before they learned how Squirrelflight and Leafpool had lied to them.

I don't know how Hollyleaf's fur got into the store, he thought, *but I should have thrown it out when I first found it there, not left it for another cat to find.*

"I wonder where it came from," Briarlight meowed. "Maybe a cat from another Clan got in here to steal herbs." She stifled a *mrrow* of laughter. "Maybe the kits got in and hid it."

"How would I know?" Jayfeather snapped, irritated at being jerked out of his memories. "You should stop letting your imagination run away with you."

Turning so that Briarlight couldn't see what he was doing, he tucked the scrap of fur deep inside the moss of his nest, and rose to his paws. "I'm going to fetch that marigold," he mewed, and headed out of the den.

ENTER THE WORLD OF

WARRIORS

Warriors

inister perils threaten the four warrior Clans. Into the midst of this turmoil mes Rusty, an ordinary housecat, who may just be the bravest of them all.

Download the new free Warriors app at www.warriorcats.com

Warriors: The New Prophecy

Follow the next generation of heroic cats as they set off on a quest to save the Clans from destruction.

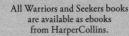 All Warriors and Seekers books are available as ebooks from HarperCollins.

 Also available unabridged from HarperChildren's*Audio*

www.warriorcats.com for the free Warriors app, games, Clan lore, and much more!